4 7340 00012776 6

D1126193

South Central Elementary Library
Union Mills, Indiana

BAKER & TAYLOR

3

GRADY'S IN THE SILO

GRADY'S IN THE SILO

Written by Una Belle Townsend
Illustrated by Bob Artley

South Central Elementary Library
Union Mills, Indiana

PELICAN PUBLISHING COMPANY
Gretna 2003

Copyright © 2003
By Una Belle Townsend

Illustrations copyright © 2003
By Bob Artley
All rights reserved

The word "Pelican" and the depiction of a pelican are trademarks
of Pelican Publishing Company, Inc., and are registered
in the U.S. Patent and Trademark Office.

Library of Congress Cataloging-in-Publication Data

Townsend, Una Belle.
  Grady's in the silo / written by Una Belle Townsend ; illustrated by
Bob Artley.
      p. cm.
Summary: Grady the Hereford cow gets stuck in the silo of Bill and
Alyne's farm in Yukon, Oklahoma. Based on an actual event that occurred
in 1949.
  ISBN 1-58980-098-2 (alk. paper)
  1. Hereford cows—Juvenile fiction. [1. Hereford cows—Fiction. 2.
Cows—Fiction. 3. Animal rescue—Fiction. 4. Farm
life—Oklahoma—Fiction. 5. Yukon (Okla.)—Fiction.] I. Artley, Bob,
ill. II. Title.
  PZ10.3.T68 Gr 2003
  [E]—dc21

                              2002012062

Printed in China
Published by Pelican Publishing Company, Inc.
1000 Burmaster Street, Gretna, Louisiana 70053

GRADY'S IN THE SILO

Bill rushed through the kitchen door. "Call the vet!"
His wife, Alyne, looked up. "Is it Grady?"
"Yes," said Bill, as he reached for the telephone. "It's cold outside, and that stubborn, wild cow is sick. We've put her in the little feed shed between the barn and the silo, where she'll be warmer. I hope Doc can help her."

Grady was one of Bill and Charley Mach's big, red, Hereford cows on the Mach farm in Yukon, Oklahoma. She enjoyed grazing in the green grass in the summer and munching on hay in the winter. However, she wasn't feeling very good at the moment.

In a little while, Bill hurried out to greet Doc as he drove up in his little black truck.

"Doc, I hope you can help Grady. She's a good cow, and I'd like to see her well again," said Bill.

Dr. Crump checked her over, told Bill that she'd soon
be feeling better, and decided to give her a shot. As soon
as he did, Grady began looking for a way to leave. She
had been cooped up in the shed long enough. She wanted out—and she wanted out *now*.

Suddenly, Grady saw some light. She thought it led
outdoors. She took a big, quick leap. She would be glad
to be free from all the humans fussing about her—but
she had a huge surprise awaiting her.

Instead of being free and out in the pasture, Grady had jumped into a strange round building. She couldn't get out. She had jumped into the *silo!*

Bill and Dr. Crump peered into the silo. "How did she get in there?" asked Bill. "I just turned around for a second. She raced past me and was gone."

"I don't know how she did it," said the vet, shaking his head. "Why, that silo's opening is no bigger than a news-paper page, and she must weigh about twelve hundred pounds! How could she squeeze through there?"

Now that she was inside the silo, Grady wanted out. She began mooing loudly as Bill and Doc stood nearby, watching her.

Finally, Dr. Crump walked toward his truck. "Bill, don't worry about her. She got herself in the silo; she'll just have to get herself out. Keep her comfortable, and make sure she has plenty of food and water."

Meanwhile, Grady paced inside the silo. She was mad, tired, and confused. She just wanted to be free in the pasture. Yet, she was stuck—stuck in this huge, tall, gray silo. How could she get out?

That evening, Bill and Alyne still couldn't believe it.
Grady continued mooing. "Oh, well," said Bill before
going to bed. "Doc seems to think that she'll get herself
out tomorrow when she calms down."

The next morning, though, Bill could still hear Grady bellowing. The vet called to see if she had squeezed her way out yet. "No," said Bill. "In fact, she kept us up half the night with her bawling." How could they get her out? they wondered.

Early that same morning, some of Bill's friends, neighbors, and a newspaper editor heard about Grady. The editor of the *Yukon Sun* told other editors, and soon, people from all over Oklahoma, as well as all over the world, knew about the Hereford in the silo. People began calling Bill to offer advice on how to rescue Grady.

Some people suggested taking strong ropes and lifting her out from the top of the silo.

South Central Elementary Library
Union Mills, Indiana

Others said that the silo should be taken down piece by piece to save the cow. Both of these suggestions meant that Grady might be hurt if something fell on her.

Bill really liked his stubborn, wild cow, and his silo was needed on the farm. He didn't want either one harmed or destroyed. What could Bill do?

Bill received many other ideas in letters and telegrams.

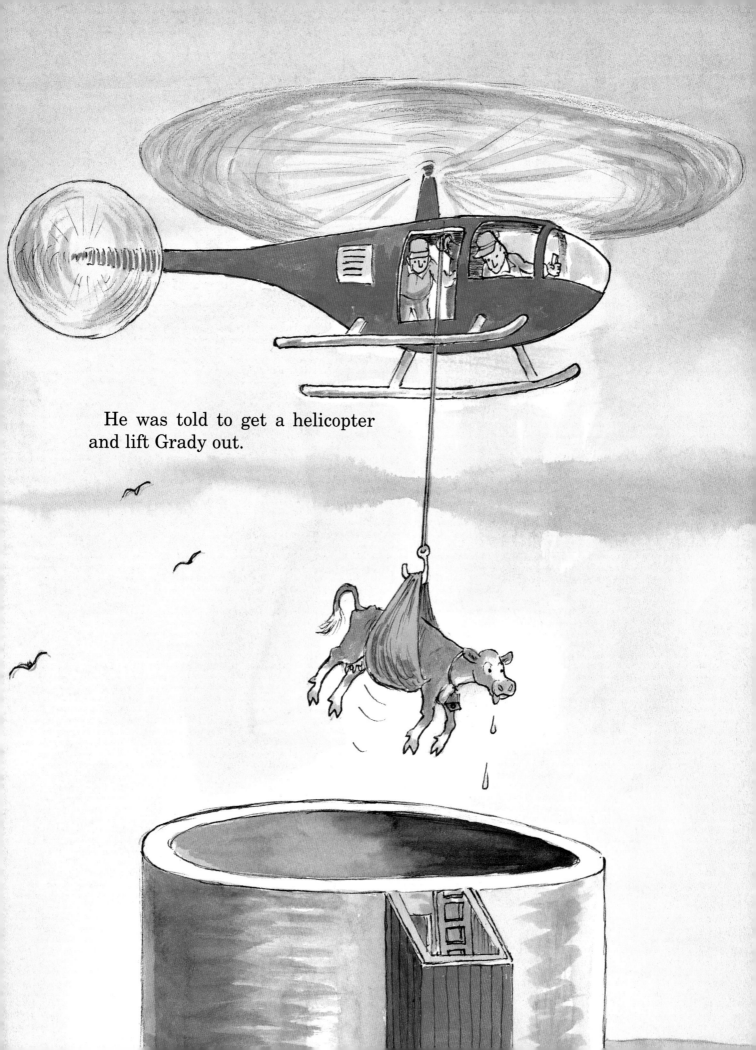

He was told to get a helicopter
and lift Grady out.

Someone said to tunnel underneath the silo and drag her out. Both ideas seemed dangerous.

Then Bill was told to fill the silo with water and float Grady to the top. How would she get down to the ground from the top of the silo? everyone wondered.

By the fourth day, Bill had received 770 telegrams from forty-five states. People in Canada, Mexico, France, and Germany had contacted him, too. Before long, thousands of letters from around the world poured in, and the phone calls were endless! The family couldn't get any sleep.

The *Yukon Sun*'s editor and the mayor were also flooded with phone calls. Anyone who couldn't talk to Bill called these men and attempted to tell them how to rescue Grady.

Meanwhile, Grady was tired. She had roamed around in circles, munched hay, and drank water. She had tried to tell Bill that she wanted out, but she was still stuck in the silo. It had been four long, miserable days for her, too.

Then a farm editor from the *Denver Post,* Ralph Partridge, called Bill. He said he wanted to fly to Yukon to get Grady out of the silo, and he knew just how to do it.

When Ralph arrived, he immediately began preparing to rescue Grady. "Bill, I think that if Dr. Crump sedates her, we can rub a big bucket of grease on her, and we can slip her out of that tiny opening," he said.

And that's just what happened. Early on the fifth morning, around three hundred people showed up to see Grady.

They watched as Bill, his brother Charley, and some friends and neighbors tried to get Grady out of her prison. Some men were in the silo pushing on Grady, who had been sedated and greased. Other men were outside the silo struggling to pull her out. All they had to do was push and pull.

Suddenly, Grady popped out.

She was free. She had spent five days in a dark prison, and now she could see the sun, the pasture, and—

oh—what a beautiful morning it was. What a beautiful
day in Yukon, Oklahoma!